John William Meaden, John Vale

The Poetical Works of John William Meaden

John William Meaden, John Vale

The Poetical Works of John William Meaden

ISBN/EAN: 9783337378943

Printed in Europe, USA, Canada, Australia, Japan

Cover: Foto ©Andreas Hilbeck / pixelio.de

More available books at **www.hansebooks.com**

THE POETICAL WORKS

OF

J. W. MEADEN

EDITED, AND WITH

BIOGRAPHICAL SKETCH,

BY

JOHN VALE.

MELBOURNE:

The Victorian Alliance, Temperance Buildings, Swanston St.
The Sunday School Union, Little Collins St.
Mr. M. L. Hutchinson, 305-7 Little Collins St.
The Temperance Book Depot, Russell St.
The Women's Christian Temperance Union, 138-40 Flinders St.

1899.

MELBOURNE:

McCARRON, BIRD AND CO., PRINTERS,

479 COLLINS STREET.

TO

CECIL H., FREDERICK W., EDITH J. AND HENRY W. MEADEN,

WHO MINISTERED TO THEIR FATHER'S

HAPPINESS IN LIFE,

AND WHO NOW WORTHILY UPHOLD THE HONOUR

OF HIS NAME,

THIS VOLUME IS DEDICATED,

WITH

RESPECT AND ADMIRATION.

INDEX.

		PAGE
ARGONAUTS, THE ...	... ...	75
AUSTRALIA, A CANTATA POEM ...	... ...	87
„ A FEDERATION HYMN	... ...	74
BIOGRAPHICAL SKETCH ...	... ...	9
CHILDREN'S GIFTS, THE ...	... ...	81
CHILDREN'S VOICES	... ...	48
CHRISTMAS EVE AT FERNSHAW ...	... ...	49
COMING MEN, THE	... ...	56
EPILOGUE, CLOSE OF GEELONG EXHIBITION ...		43
EVENTIDE, AT	... ...	61
FAREWELL. ...	... ...	111
HENRY KENDALL, IN MEMORIAM	... ...	67
HOMAGE TO OUR QUEEN ...	... ...	72
INAUGURAL POEM, ADELAIDE TEMPERANCE CON-		
VENTION	... ...	46
LINES SUGGESTED BY GLASS STEAM ENGINE		58
MESSAGE OF THE SWAN, THE ...	... ...	60
MUSINGS IN THE MELBOURNE PICTURE GALLERY:		
I BUNYAN IN PRISON	... ...	92
II ANGUISH ...	... ...	93
III THE FIRST SNOW ...	... ...	95
IV DRUIDICAL MONUMENTS ...	... ...	96
V THE PILGRIM FATHERS ...	... ...	97

INDEX

	PAGE
"Not as Those Without Hope"	64
Nuptial Wish, A	68
Orange Lily in Australia, The	62
Prologue, "Ye Olde English Fayre" ...	65
Soul Wings	55
Temperance Hymns and Poems:	
Prologue — International Temperance	
Conference	99
Almighty Friend	101
The Sons of Rechab	102
The Victorian Alliance Hymn	105
The Victorian Alliance War Song ...	106
A Hymn	108
Australian Temperance Hymn	109
Vote as You Pray	110
"There Shall be no More Sea"	69
To My Niece	80
Tribute, A	7
Verse on Some Shells	66
Victoria, Opening of the Melbourne Inter-	
national Exhibition, 1880-1	35
Victoria's Song of Praise	71
Welcome, Opening of Geelong Exhibition	40
Youthful Toilers	83

A TRIBUTE

TO J. W. MEADEN

I KNOW not if the absence of desire
  Hath wholly won thee from the beaten way,
  Or if thine eyes have sought the heights
    alway
Where, loving truth, the happiest aspire;
I know not if upon pale passion's pyre
  Are set the bygone hopes of some sweet
    day,
  Whose ghost thy life has haunted. This I
    say,
"Thy life is nobleness!" What praise is higher?
For nobleness is that great light which throws
  A ringing radiance round our darkened days,
    A glory that redeems our fallen state;
For it begets all virtue, and it glows
  More glorious than imperishable bays
    Untouched beyond insuperable fate.

J. B. O'HARA

"Songs of the South"
Second Edition

JOHN WILLIAM MEADEN.

JOHN WILLIAM MEADEN was born in London on the 12th of August in the year 1840.   He was a descendant of one of the families who came over, not with William the Conqueror, but with that later William who was a conqueror in the good cause of " A Free Parliament and the Protestant Religion."

Mr. Meaden's early years were spent at Camberwell, which was at the time one of the pleasantest outskirts of southern London, where his father had retired to enjoy leisure after securing a competency from his business as a city publisher and bookseller.   He received the first part of his education at an academy presided over by one Richard Crowder, who was esteemed as a worthy man and a good teacher.   His studies were continued at St. John's College, Hurstpierpoint, Sussex, with success, to which a number of valuable prizes, emblazoned with the college motto, bear eloquent testimony.   He left the college for the arena of life's battle earlier than was usual with those in his station, but he had the satisfaction of knowing that he had made the best use of the opportunities of education afforded to him.

It was at St. John's College that the spark of poetic fire burst into flame. Some early compositions from Mr. Meaden's pen were copied by his mother in her scrap book. In that kindly haven they were preserved from the fate which befel many of the later pieces, con-cerning which the author said, "they flared up splen-didly." The first piece preserved in the mother's writing is headed, "My own darling Willie's first composition, sent to me by him, 11th April, 1853. Willie in his thirteenth year." It is a vivid description of May-day festivities, as they were carried out in English villages at the time, including the raising of the May-pole—

All decked with flowers and ribbons gay.

Another piece, "The Proposal," describes how—

We parted then, but found it hard
To tear ourselves away.

As the author was not fourteen, we may assume that the lines were not autobiographical, but merely dis-played a happy faculty of entering into the feelings of others. Some lines on "Christmas Morn," with a foot-note by the mother, throw a bright side light upon the characters of both mother and son. The note reads, "God bless my darling boy! May he ever have the fervent heart to inspire him in his Lord's holy way, and guide him at last to his heavenly rest." Happy mother, to have her heart's dearest wish for her boy so abun-dantly realised as it was!

In 1854, before reaching the age of fourteen, Mr. Meaden left his native land, alone, and going first to the Brazils, visiting Monte Video and Rio de Janeiro, arrived eventually at Melbourne by way of the dreaded Cape Horn, on board the *Twee Gezusters*. Some verses written during the voyage betoken that fervent patriotism and love of home which absence usually engenders—

> I dearly love Old England,
> The sweetest isle on earth.

In the old world, exciting, though inglorious, things were happening. The French usurper sought that unstable thing called glory to strengthen his unstable throne, and Britain was in unholy alliance with him in seeking to perpetuate the blighting power of the Turk in Europe. But the popular imagination was struck more by the deeds of reckless daring on the battle field, than by the blunders and the crimes of rulers; and Tennyson was not the only poet who sang of the wild charge of the Light Brigade. And, maybe, an English mother who received some verses in praise of the heroes from her boy in Collingwood, in distant Victoria, and who treasured them in her scrap book, thought that they were not excelled even by the stirring lines of the great laureate. Some verses on " The Dead Czar," by the youthful poet, indicate a more charitable view of the adversary than was popular at the time.

The colony of Victoria was young when Mr. Meaden landed on its shores. Only three years before, separation from New South Wales had been hailed with wild delight. Less than twenty years before, the first house

was erected on the site of the future capital. The year
of Mr. Meaden's arrival saw responsible government
consummated by the passing of the Constitution Act.
It was the year, too, of the founding of municipal
institutions. Disorder was in evidence as well as order,
for it was the year of the Eureka Stockade. Mr.
Meaden had a poet's insight of the future. He realised
that he was privileged to take part in the founding of
an important community. He saw visions of a vast
population, with lives brightened by the sunlight of
material prosperity in larger measure than was the
case in the old lands, and in more general enjoyment of
the beneficent influences of education, and of leisure
which could be the mother of culture; and he ardently
desired that the greatness of the coming people should
have as its crown the righteousness which exalteth a
nation. He knew the widespread influence of strong
drink in preventing the realisation of similar aspirations
in other lands, and patriotically resolved to serve his
adopted country by at once enlisting with the soldiers
of abstinence. It was chiefly as a Christian patriot that
he became an abstainer from alcohol.

Mr. Meaden's independent business career began
while he was in his teens. In 1863 he was married to
Marianne, fifth daughter of Mr. A. Bullock, of Dungan-
non, in the north of Ireland. For thirty-five years he
enjoyed with her, in unusual measure—

> Domestic happiness, the only bliss
> Of Paradise that has survived the fall.

His home and business premises were in Wellington-
street, Collingwood, which at that time promised to be

the leading business thoroughfare of a flourishing suburb. During early manhood the limited leisure of an active business life was devoted to temperance, Sabbath school, and church work, and in some measure to literary pursuits. Some prose contributions to the local press and other papers are preserved, but the poetry of this period appears to have been material for the "flare up" previously mentioned. At the time of the general election of 1880 Mr. Meaden was strongly urged by many who knew his sterling character and appreciated his abilities as a speaker and thinker, to allow himself to be nominated for the representation of Collingwood. He declined, even without reluctance. Probably for his own peace of mind it was well that he did. He was too modest and retiring for the hurly-burly of political life. And yet it is a leavening with men of Mr. Meaden's stamp that Parliament urgently needs.

In 1879 an Industrial and Juvenile Exhibition was opened at Geelong. A prize was offered for the best poem to be spoken as a prologue at the opening ceremony. In connection with the Exhibition the united total abstinence societies of Geelong offered a gold medal as a prize for the best essay " On the Benefits of Total Abstinence from Intoxicating Liquors." Mr. Meaden won both prizes. He had achieved a similar success in several other literary competitions. His crowning triumph in the literary arena followed quickly. In connection with the Melbourne International Exhibition of 1880, the ceremonial committee offered a premium of 50 guineas for the best poem to be sung as a cantata at the opening. There were 198 competitors in the different colonies, including Mr. Meaden, to whom the prize was awarded. The selected poem was set to music by M. Leon Caron, and was rendered at the opening of the Exhibition, on 1st October, by a choir and orchestra of 1000 performers, with the leading Melbourne vocalists as principals. The impression was overwhelming, and the author and composer were presented to the Governor, the Marquis of Normanby, amid the enthusiastic plaudits of the vast audience of 20,000 persons. The poem was described as one of the best things about the Exhibition, and, in recognition of its superior merit, the author was awarded a gold medal in addition to the monetary prize. This success brought Mr. Meaden to the front in public life. His services as a speaker came to be in great demand. As much as 2s. was paid for admission to hear his popular lecture on "The Journey of Life," the proceeds going to charitable objects, and in all the advertisements and reports he was referred to as "the author of the Exhibition Cantata."

In connection with the Exhibition an International Temperance Conference was held in Melbourne at the Temperance Hall, beginning on 9th November. Mr. Meaden wrote a poem which was spoken as the prologue to the conference. In the course of the proceedings the late Hon. W. M. K. Vale moved a resolution, which was adopted, in favour of the formation in each of the colonies of an Alliance on lines similar to those of the United Kingdom Alliance for the Suppression of the Liquor Traffic. Victoria was the first to give effect to this. All the other colonies of Australasia have followed. On 10th February, 1881, a committee was formed to arrange the preliminaries for the projected organisation. On 17th May following, the inaugural meeting of the Victorian Alliance was held at the Melbourne Temperance Hall. An executive committee was elected, which subsequently appointed Mr. Meaden as the secretary of the new association. The duties of the office were entered upon with characteristic zeal, including the holding of Alliance meetings in the suburbs, and in some parts of the country. Cordial press notices of Mr. Meaden's addresses remain, showing that the infant association was happy in the medium who voiced its first appeals for public support.

Soon after the inception of the Alliance Mr. Meaden established the *Alliance Record* as the organ of the association. The first number of the journal saw the light on 15th October, 1881. For several years Mr. Meaden was the editor of this paper, and he was always a contributor to its pages. In establishing the paper he saw that it would serve as a bond of union between the members of the Alliance who would be scattered over the colony, and would be unable to meet together at short intervals, as the members of temperance organisations having local branches are supposed to do. In the light of experience we can see that this anticipation has been abundantly fulfilled.

On 24th May, 1882, a Queen's Birthday celebration took place in the Melbourne Exhibition Building. In connection with this event a prize was offered for the best essay upon " The Life of the Queen of England," the composition being limited to 500 words. Thirty-one essays were received, and the one selected by the judges as the best proved to be from the pen of Mr. Meaden, to whom the prize was accordingly awarded. The essay was printed and distributed amongst those who attended the celebration.

In the middle part of 1882 the writer first saw Mr. Meaden. On 27th July in that year, he was appointed to the Alliance secretaryship, which Mr. Meaden desired to relinquish. Mr. Meaden was elected as the hon. secretary, and continued for a time the editorship of the *Alliance Record*. It is with singular emotion that I write of these changes. They marked the beginning of a friendship which ripened with the passing years, and was true to death. After nearly seventeen years of close comradeship I could say, in the words of John Bright regarding Richard Cobden, " I little knew how much I loved him until I found that I had lost him."

During the year 1883 Mr. Meaden removed to Albert Park, where he carried on business in Bridport-street West. He became an active member of the Albert Park Presbyterian Church, and continued also to devote time and energy to the temperance cause, to Sabbath-school work, and to other philanthropic agencies. Occasionally, too, he added to his literary laurels. In 1886 he won two prizes, each of £50. One was given by the proprietors of the "Australasian Federal Directory" for the best essay on "The Commercial Development of Australasia." The other was given by the proprietors of the " Year Book of Australia" in Sydney for the best essay on the subject of "A Protectionist Policy for the Colony of Victoria." In these two efforts the writer, it was understood, was in competition with some of the best literary talent of Australia, and it was no small thing to achieve success in both.

The following is from the opening paragraph of the essay on "The Commercial Development of Australasia":—"Just a century ago, in the year 1788, the first English settlers landed upon the shores of the continent of Australia. These were mainly exiled outcasts, who came in bonds to found a home for freedom. They brought with them amidst their sins, their sorrows, and their shame, some better things, some characteristics of the race from which they had been roughly separated by the hand of justice. The rude outlines which they marked out upon these then savage coasts were traced in accordance with the traditions of the land from which they came, and from which were drawn in after years the true founders of Australasia; for these convict settlers were not the fathers of the communities which now flourish under the Southern Cross. They were pioneers, few in number, and destined soon to lose their individuality amidst the great waves of voluntary immigration that followed in their wake. With their coming, however, commences the history of Australasia, which, like mighty Rome, began as an asylum for lawbreakers." This puts the "birth-stain" in a new, and kindly, light.

In 1887 a long cherished desire of Mr. Meaden's to visit the "dear home land" was gratified. Prior to his departure a farewell social gathering was held at the Victoria Coffee Palace, on 11th February. The Hon. W. M. K. Vale, who was one of the closest personal friends of the guest, presided. An address, handsomely illuminated on vellum and bound in morocco, was presented to Mr. Meaden, testifying to the high esteem in which he was held by the Victorian Alliance and the allied societies as a talented writer and speaker, a good citizen, a faithful friend, and a devoted Christian worker. Speeches of a highly eulogistic character were delivered by members of Parliament, personal friends of the guest, and prominent workers in the temperance cause, all of which voiced the feelings of the many present, whose well-loved faces were, after all, the best proof of wide-spread esteem. Mr. Meaden travelled by way of Hobart to New Zealand, and saw many of the weird beauties of the sounds, lakes, and mountains of that delightful wonderland. Crossing the great Pacific, he renewed acquaintance with the tropical scenery of Brazil, and the world's finest harbour at Rio de Janeiro. Travelling northward, he was soon able to exclaim with delight—

This is my own, my native land.

A gap of thirty-three years had severed many early friends from knowledge, but he renewed acquaintance with some who were loved in the long ago, and who remembered his father and him. He was welcomed by many of the leaders in temperance and philanthropy, and spoke in the historic Exeter Hall in company with a baroness, an earl, and a bishop. Ireland and Scotland were visited, the former country having peculiar attraction as the home of Mrs. Meaden's people. A trip to the Continent included " La Belle France," the blue waters of the Rhine, the mountains of Switzerland, and the classic grounds of Italy. The homeward route was by way of the Suez Canal and Colombo, so that when the traveller returned he had been round the world. A popular lecture, " There and Back," delivered by Mr. Meaden, conveyed pleasure and infor-

mation to many audiences, and made his journey profit-
able to the funds of some deserving institutions.

In 1888 Mr. Meaden accepted the position of corresponding secretary to the Victorian Alliance, taking
charge of the office and literary work in order to leave
the other secretary more available for country engage-
ments. In connection with the International Exhibition
of that year an International Temperance Convention
was held in Melbourne. The arrangements were
carried out by a large and representative committee.
Mr. Meaden was elected as one of three hon. secre-
taries. The Convention proved to be the largest and
most representative body of temperance workers ever
assembled beneath the Southern Cross. To Mr.
Meaden was accorded the honour of reading the opening paper, which was entitled "Temperance in Australia." The concluding words of the paper were
expressive of the bright hopefulness which always
animated the writer :—" Our progress may be comparatively slow, the day of our complete deliverance may be
long delayed, but we have progressed, we are still
advancing, and the day shall come when He who hath
led us thus far on our upward way shall crown, not us,
perhaps, but those who shall rise up to take our places,
with victory, and shall plant the standard of temperance on the heights where it may float above Australian lands, from whence the drink shop has been
banished, and where drunkenness and its attendant
miseries are no more known." Mr. Meaden was the
editor of the memorial volume of the Convention which
received the title of his opening paper. This was the
largest temperance work ever issued in Australia, and it

deserved a wider measure of support than that which was accorded to it.

Mr. Meaden had enjoyed his journey "there and back" so much that he determined to give Mrs. Meaden similar pleasures, and in 1890, having relinquished his position as corresponding secretary of the Alliance, he took her on a trip to Europe, which afforded, amongst other privileges, the opportunity of reunion with her own people. Prior to their departure they shared in a farewell social gathering at the Melbourne Coffee Palace, held in their honour, and also that of other departing temperance friends.

Mr. Meaden had cherished several dreams. One was that of freedom from business cares, with leisure devoted to philanthropy and to literary pursuits. Shortly after his return from the second journey to Europe, this desire seemed realised. He retired to Surrey Hills to a house designed and built for himself. But the horrible Frankenstein, which Melbourne called into being by the land boom, and which converted even prudent investments into hopeless liabilities, hung over him during the period of retirement, and finally dashed his hopes to pieces. He could have said with truth, "All is lost save honour," and with cheerfulness he returned to resume the burdens of business life. Had the leisure been free from anxiety, and longer, the impression made by Mr. Meaden in public life would have been deeper, and the literary legacy left behind would have been richer than it is.

Mr. Meaden was devoted to work amongst the young. He realised that in raising a barrier between the wine cup and the unpolluted lips of the little ones lay one of the chief hopes of the temperance movement. In May, 1891, he established the Picture and Lantern Mission for the purpose of utilising the pictorial method of disseminating temperance truth, especially amongst the young. In Melbourne and its outskirts, in the provincial cities and towns, and in many of the smaller and remote settlements, the light of truth was conveyed to the mind in the most effective way by the illustrated lectures. Both the young and the grown-up flock listened and looked with pleasure, and certainly in many cases with lasting benefit. The Mission was inaugurated as an auxiliary to the Band of Hope Union, in which the promoter took a deep interest; and when that deserving institution ceased to exist it was continued in connection with the Victorian Alliance. After Mr. Meaden's death his elder sons, Messrs. C. H. and F. W. Meaden, generously gave to the Alliance the lantern, slides, and other effects, which are of considerable value, believing, that in thus providing for the continuance of the work, they were acting in accordance with their father's wishes.

The Sunday School Union shared in Mr. Meaden's unbounded interest in the young. For several years he acted as visitor for the Union, and occasionally contributed papers to teachers' conferences which displayed appreciation of the importance of the teacher's calling and knowledge of the needs of the teacher's work. The Sunday Schools' Industrial Exhibition, held in the Melbourne Exhibition Building in October, 1896, was opened with an ode—" Youthful Toilers"—which Mr. Meaden wrote for the occasion, and which was set to music by Dr. M'Burney. It was rendered by a large choir with success, which recalled a triumph with which the author was associated, in the same building, sixteen years before. A unique feature of the Diamond Jubilee celebrations, in 1897, was a Sunday-school demonstration, held in the Exhibition Building on 25th June. The capacity of Melbourne's largest hall was taxed as it never had been, 20,000 scholars and teachers being present, besides the leading choir of 1200 members, and the audience, which included Lord and Lady Brassey. Mr. Meaden had written for the occasion a hymn, entitled " Homage to Our Queen," and set to the tune of " The March of the Men of Harlech." The rendering of this by the more than 20,000 voices, to the accompaniment of as many Union Jacks waved in unison by the singers, was one of the finest parts of a unique programme. Both the scene and the sound were most inspiring, and loud cheers were evoked from the audience.

From waving flags, the strains of fresh young voices, youthful hearts pulsating with hope, and faces radiant with anticipation, to the death-bed and the grave seems a long step, but it is the one I have to take in this brief record. For some months a darker shadow than that of impending financial loss, endured at Surrey Hills, hung over the home at Albert Park—the shadow of death. And the stricken one was dearer to our friend than life itself. It is rarely that we see a couple so happily mated as Mr. and Mrs. Meaden were. In the ideal marriage there is a sense in which the two literally become one. These two were one—

As perfect music unto noble words.

Mrs. Meaden met with an accident while out with her husband on a wedding-day holiday, which for some months deprived her of the use of her right arm. This was followed by a painful illness which was borne not merely with courage and patience, but with cheerfulness. Near the end her sufferings ceased, and she seemed to pass into the better life even before she left this. One thing happened which seems wonderful. She was devoted to the service of the sanctuary and regular in her attendance at the week-night services. But she could uot join in the singing. This she felt to be a real loss to herself. She could not sing. And yet before she passed to the better land she sang three hymns so sweetly that to her dear ones who listened it seemed as though the gates of heaven were opened, and that they were catching the echo of angel strains. And so in peace and joy the pure spirit went to God. The manner of the passing away took the sting from death, and left sweet drops in the cup of bitterness.

Mrs. Meaden died on 17th July, 1898, and her mortal remains were buried in the Melbourne General Cemetery on 19th July. She had—

Allured to brighter worlds, and led the way.

For several weeks prior to her death, Mr. Meaden had no rest. The sufferer was subject to sudden paroxysms of pain, and her husband, better than anyone else, could hold her hands and soothe her. And so he remained by her side night and day for weeks. After the death the inevitable reaction from the prolonged strain, on a physical nature by no means strong, was terrible. The grief of the parting was bravely borne, but the bodily injury was irreparable. Mr.

Meaden settled down to the old duties under the changed conditions, contentedly and cheerfully show-ing—

How sublime a thing it is
To suffer and be strong.

But it was easy to see that the chief interest was centred in the land "which is far better." One who was accustomed to hear him at this period in public prayer described the effect produced as being as though "a voice from the other world were speaking." He was with us, but not of us.

The excessive physical strain he had undergone had occasioned heart trouble, of which he had several serious warnings. On the morning of Monday, March 20th, 1899, he fell on the floor at home unconscious and apparently dead. Under medical treatment he rallied a little, but at half-past one the next morning, March 21st, he passed peacefully away. His last words, spoken to his only daughter, were "Good night, darling." For him it was the dawn of a beautiful good morning. Within eight brief months two kindred souls were reunited. "They were lovely and pleasant in their lives and in their death they were not" long "divided."

The sad duty of consigning the remains of our friend to the tomb was performed on the afternoon of March 22nd. The Albert Park Presbyterian Church, in which only three days before the departed one had worshipped, was filled with mourners, and an impressive service was conducted by the Rev. F. E. Oxer, M.A., the pastor. Mr. J. W. Hunt, the chairman of the Victorian Alliance, spoke in eulogy of the departed, with

 Mrs. J. W. Meaden.

whom he had been happily associated in temperance work for more than sixteen years. The pastor spoke of the high Christian standard of Mr. Meaden's every-day life, and of the loss which the church had sustained by his death. The mourners then followed the remains of the departed to their last resting place in the Melbourne General Cemetery. The service at the grave was conducted by the Revs. F. E. Oxer and A. MacDonald M.A., the latter of Surrey Hills.

The following is the text of the Rev. F. E. Oxer's address:—" Jesus said ' Suffer the little children to come unto Me and forbid them not, for of such is the Kingdom of Heaven;' and such was he whose poor clay we commit to the earth to-day. He had weathered the storms of life and reached the haven of a calm trust and simple childlike obedience. He had lost the unrest, but not the enthusiasm, of youth. His spirit was bright and buoyant; his heart tender and loving. His life had shown us how to enjoy prosperity, and how to meet adversity; it assures us that the humble believer may aspire to be what Paul was when he said ' I have learned in whatsoever state I am, therewith to be content. I know how to be abased and I know how to abound. I can do all things through Christ who strengtheneth me.' He had a call from God to wage war with one of the worst enemies that threaten our national life—the demon Intemperance, that snatches bread from the mouths of the poor and blights the prosperity of the rich. In cloud and sunshine alike the sword was ever in his hand, and he died in harness. Such a life is a monument of the power of Christ to redeem, a treasure to the Church, an inspiration to us all."

Some traits of Mr. Meaden's beautiful character have been portrayed in the course of this brief sketch. There are several which demand enlargement. Mr. Frederic Smith, of London, who has been for many years foremost in connection with the work of the United Kingdom Band of Hope Union, wrote of our friend:—
" I am very sorry that his life has terminated at a com-paratively early age, for his kind is greatly needed. I am glad I had the privilege of making his acquaintance when he was in England, at which time I was greatly drawn to him. He seemed so gentle, and yet so strong, and his devotion to work amongst the young appears to have been maintained to the end. I trust that his example will stimulate many, but how few there are in this money-getting age who are prepared, as he was, to throw themselves into the work."

" So gentle, and yet so strong." This impression from a comparatively brief acquaintance was intensified with those who were privileged to labour side by side with Mr. Meaden for many years. The qualities at their best are not opposites. They spring from, and are made kindred by, love.

One of Mr. Meaden's characteristics is but rarely associated with the poetic temperament. I refer to thoroughness. A paper which he read at a teachers' conference, in connection with the Sunday School Union, in 1886, opened as follows:—" That ' whatever is worth doing at all is worth doing well ' is an old-fashioned axiom dear to the hearts of all English-speaking people. The truth which it contains has been inculcated into the hearts of generations that have passed away from earth, but which have left the impress of their lives and characters not simply upon the records of the days in which they lived, but also in-scribed indelibly upon the hearts and consciences of those whom they called their children and trained to follow in their footsteps. Of all the qualities on which an Englishman is prone to pride himself, *thoroughness* ranks among the first, and it was because the thoroughness that was in his nature stamped itself upon everything that passed through his hands that the workmanship of Englishmen gained for itself a fame that spread far beyond the limits of their island home, and England became the foremost manufacturing nation of the earth. It was the thoroughness of the English character that has caused the English flag to fly above so many widely scattered portions of the world's surface, and that has given the army of England —numerically small though it may be—a name and a place amongst the military forces of the earth."

The writer then proceeded to apply the lesson to the sacred calling of the Sunday-school teacher, and in this regard, as in others, his life exemplified his precept.

Thoroughness was characteristic of his advocacy of the temperance cause. The modern schemes for throw-ing the white robe of righteousness over the iniquitous liquor traffic found in him an uncompromising opponent. He said, speaking of the Victorian Alliance:—" We have no plan to submit by which the liquor traffic shall be so restricted that it shall become beneficial, no method of regulation which can allow it to exist and yet be harm-less, no mode of palliation which shall make its woes tolerable. We cannot frame any scheme by which the community can at once serve God and mammon, or

enjoy the profits of the manufacture and sale of drink
without being involved in the miseries they entail. We
can offer to the community the boon of freedom from
the evils of intemperance only on condition of the abso-
lute and complete abolition of the liquor traffic.

" In this idea of prohibition lies the hope of our movement, and, in large measure, of the future happiness
and prosperity of our people. In no irreverent spirit,
therefore, I venture to apply to it the description given
to the infinitely greater means of a still greater deliverance. It is to some 'a stumbling block,' to others
' foolishness,' but in it, and in it alone, there is for our
land, we believe, ' the power of God unto salvation,'
rom the evils wrought by strong drink. To prepare
the community for the renunciation it involves is the
main purpose of all our educational work. To place in
the hands of the members of the community the means
of carrying this renunciation into effect is the great aim
of all our schemes of legislative reform. When these
great objects shall be accomplished, when public
opinion and legislative enactment shall, in happy
unison, be directed to the abolition of the most
disastrous and destructive traffic that ever afflicted
humanity, then, and not till then, shall our land rise to
the full measure of its prosperity. Then to our clearer
skies, no longer polluted by the reek of the brewery and
the distillery, shall arise the incense of the happy
homes of an entirely sober and, therefore, prosperous
people ; the tavern doors shall vomit forth no more
their myriad streams of muddled sots ; the midnight air
be no more burdened with the cries of shrieking wives
and of affrighted children, but the Southern Cross,

enshrined amidst the twinkling stars, shall shine over a peaceful land where God's law is honoured, where man is blest, and where the drunkard and the drunkard maker are alike unknown."

The vices are kindred, as well as the virtues. Mr. Meaden recognised this truth, and battled with gambling and impurity as making, with intemperance, "A Trinity of Evil." In the course of the paper read at the teachers' conference, from which I have before quoted, he wrote:—" If there are many strange things in the Bible, there are also many strange things in human life. There are terrible dangers and pitfalls which beset the young, the ignorant, the innocent, and the unwary. In this connection I believe that upon the teachers of our senior classes there devolves a grave responsibility. Many a brave young life has been blasted, many a pure young heart has, I believe, been carried down to worse than death for the want of the warning word which a loving teacher might have spoken, or the guiding hand which a teacher might have held out. Let me remind you of your privileges. A male teacher among his young men, a female teacher among her young women, have opportunities for enforcing moral truths and unmasking moral dangers, of attacking the foulness of earth and hell from the impregnable standpoint of Christ's spotless purity. Let me ask you to follow up these few thoughts in the spirit of the Master. He went down to the depths to lift up the fallen and degraded. Is it too great a thing to ask you to do all that in you lies to girdle round the innocent and pure with all the safeguards which His loving care has provided in His Holy Word?"

Our friend's gifts were versatile. He had a fund of original humour, which was in keeping with his cheerful spirit. His closest friends were occasionally permitted to see humorous verses written *apropos* to some passing event. Only a few of these escaped his hands to be preserved. Asked to contribute to a visitors' book at Marysville, he sat down and wrote :—

I.

Why should I stay to write a lay,
   Which none may think worth readin',
No words can grace so fair a place,
   Its beauties all concedin'.

II.

No need to tell of ferny dell,
   Or walk to Steve's falls leadin',
Or mountains grand on every hand
   In lofty tiers recedin'.

.   .   .   .   .   .

VI.

If health should cheer another year,
   And all things else accedin',
He'll come again to banish pain,
   And fetch up Mrs. Meaden.

VII.

Remember then, ye married men,
   Your selfish habits weedin',
Regard your vows, bring each your spouse,
   Ye Adams, to this Eden.

VIII.

No serpent vile shall here beguile,
   And tho' perchance indeed an
Occasional snake appearance make,
   There's few, I'm told, now breedin'.

IX.

Like Eve and Adam, Sir and Madam,
  In innocence proceedin',
May one and all, "before the fall,"*
  Soon stand with joy exceedin'.

There is no need to dilate upon Mr. Meaden's literary abilities. The fact that almost without exception when he competed for prizes, for either poetical or prose compositions, he was successful is a unique tribute. The work of composition was a joy to him, and he did his best without regard whatever to the material reward in prospect. He belonged to—

> The poets, who on earth have made us heirs
> Of truth and pure delight by heavenly lays.

The poetical productions of his later years will be found in the following pages, and they will speak for themselves. In amplification of their merit it should be remembered that they were written amid the incessant calls of a busy life. One of the choicest of the pieces, the "In Memoriam" poem to Henry Kendall, expresses our feelings for the writer—

> His harp lies shattered now—
> Silent and broken! It is fit that we
> Should weep in silence, for we have no voice
> As sweet as his to sing his elegy.

* Stevenson's Falls.

"AT REST"

"For so He giveth His beloved sleep."

WHEN the long-hoped-for hour has come at
    last,
When the long-sought-for bourne at length is
    past,
When the sweet sleep I long for shall be
    mine,
And I have found the rest for which I pine,
  Fold my pale hands across my placid breast,
  Smile as you kiss your weary one at rest.

When this sad tired heart has ceased to beat,
And I in peace have "gathered up my feet:"
When the last pang hath racked my quivering
    frame
And death's cold flood hath quenched the
    vital flame,
  Stand not in grief beside my quiet bed,
  No bitter, hopeless tears above me shed.

"AT REST"

Though my pale brow shall be as marble cold,
And pallid bonds my weary limbs enfold;
Though from my cheek the flush of life hath
    paled,
And starless night my aching eyeballs veiled,
  Shut not the sunlight from the silent room,
  While I am with you shroud me not in
  gloom.

Gladly I'll hail the night that comes with
  balm,
Pass from life's stormy seas to endless calm;
Each jarring note my quivering heart-strings
  made
Silenced by God's soft hand upon them laid.
  Sweetly I'll sleep as on my mother's breast,
  So glad, so glad to be at last "at rest."

J. W. MEADEN.

POEMS

VICTORIA

CANTATA POEM

*Sung at the Opening of the Melbourne International
Exhibition, 1880-1*

PART I—THE PAST

THE ARGUMENT.—Victoria, sleeping amidst the primeval solitudes,
is aroused by voices which foretell the speedy discovery and settle-
ment of the country, and presently the songs of the mariners are
heard as they make their way across the ocean to the, as yet,
undiscovered land—

IN slumbers deep—where branching fern-trees
    wave,
And Austral seas the long, low beaches lave,
Where fringed with reeds, the silent, lone
    lagoon
Reflects the starry cross and crescent moon,
With garner'd sweetness in her peaceful breast,
The fair Victoria lies too long at rest.

    O summer land of silence,
      O land of beauty rare,
    Where solitude lies brooding
      O'er hills and valleys fair;
    Where silent streams are stealing
      O'er each untrodden plain,
    And the lonely shores but echo
      The sigh of the surging main.

35

On thy sweet peace intruding
　The old world soon will pour
An army, vast and busy,
　Forth from its teeming shore.
And to thy pleasant harbours,
　That now all lonely lie,
"As the doves unto their windows"
　Shall the white-winged vessels fly.

Then, fair South Land, no longer
　Thy coasts shall silent be,
The merry voice of laughter
　Shall echo songs of glee.
Then busy sounds of labour
　Shall rise on the summer air,
And sweetly chime the Sabbath bell,
　That calls to the house of prayer.

THE MARINERS' SONG

Our northern homes we leave behind,
　To seek some golden strand,
Our sails we trim to catch the wind,
　And steer for the southern land.
O'er glittering seas we gaily glide
Where the sunbeams dance on the laughing
　　tide.

When storms arise their wrath we brave,
   Nor fear the lightning's flash,
Though madd'ning winds around us rave,
   And the surging billows dash,
O'er unknown seas we fearless sail
Where the Storm-fiend rides on the hissing
      gale.

PART II—THE PRESENT

THE ARGUMENT.—Victoria discovered engaged in various pursuits
—pastoral, agricultural, industrial, &c. – is approached by a company
of nymphs, representing the various nations of the earth. They hail
her with acclamation as the "Queen of the South." Victoria re-
sponds with a jubilant song of welcome, and, as she leads her guests
to the banquet, the people burst forth into a patriotic hymn, with
which the cantata concludes.

Now, on the grassy plains the browsing flocks
      descend,
While Ceres' toiling swains her fruitful reign
      extend;
Deep in the gloomy mine the digger seeks
      his prize;
Neath Labour's sway benign the fair domed
      cities rise ;
And all around we see a power subdue the
      land,
A power from God that nerves the toiler's
      willing hand.

37

CHORUS OF THE NATIONS.

From distant shores we come to greet
With loud acclaim, our sister sweet,
And hail her, as with queenly grace
Amidst our band she takes her place,
    "Queen of the Southern Seas."

VICTORIA'S SONG OF WELCOME

O golden day of glory! O chrysolite of time!
Now fly all shadows hoary before a dawn
    sublime,
Now clad in golden sunlight a bride adorn'd
    I stand,
My dowry, England's birthright, her banner
    in my hand.

O welcome! Sisters gracious, and friends
    from every land!
My heart warms at your coming to this bright
    and sunny strand.
My banquet-hall is furnished, my table richly
    spread,
The grand old flag, with star-gems deck'd,
    gleams brightly overhead.

Wave, wave your silken banners! your silver
    trumpets blow!
Sing, sing your loud hosannas! that all the
    world may know
This day is born a Nation, 'neath England's
    banner free,
That, like a constellation, flames o'er the
    Southern Sea.

HYMN

O Thou, whose arm hath for our fathers
    fought,
Whose guiding hand their sons has hither
    brought
Lead onward, till Australia's land shall rise
A Greater Britain, 'neath these southern
    skies.

With bounteous hand our fields with plenty
    bless,
Increase our flocks, our homes with peace
    possess ;
Make wise our rulers, and in righteous ways
Guide Thou our feet, to Thine eternal praise.

WELCOME

A PROLOGUE

Spoken by the Author at the Opening Ceremonial of the Geelong Industrial and Juvenile Exhibition, 1879-80

"OH, for a muse of fire!" or better still,
The power that lurked in some old poet's quill,
Then would we sing in high exultant strains
Our joy at this reward of all our pains,
This bright dispersal of our doubts and fears,
These sights and sounds that greet our eyes
     and ears,
This glad fruition of each hope that soars,
And dies content, fulfilled in your applause.

But first our hearts would welcome ev'ry friend
Who shares our joy, or comes his aid to lend
And join the song of gratitude we owe
To Him in Heaven, who rules on Earth below.
To Him from Whom alone comes all success,
Whose smile we crave our plans of love to bless,
With thankful hearts and cheerful voice we
     raise
An anthem glad of mingled love and praise.

We bid you welcome, friends, within these
    walls,
We bid you welcome to these fairy halls,
Which, like Aladdin's home, in Arab story,
That in one night arose in sudden glory,
Have quickly risen, where on either hand,
Corio's wavelets kiss the silv'ry strand,
And Barwon's waters in their tranquil flow
With golden sheen of summer sunsets glow.

Quickly these walls have grown, for ev'ry hand
Hath willing wrought the scheme so deftly
    plann'd
And quickly plenished, all our courts are graced
With works of Beauty, Industry, and Taste.
How speeds the task when all as one conspire,
When kindred wishes ev'ry heart inspire,
When kindly feelings ev'ry bosom fill,
And ev'ry hand assists with right goodwill.

Our thanks are due, those thanks we gladly pay,
To all who've help'd the triumph of to-day,
To each good friend, whose willing hands have
    wrought,
Each gen'rous heart that gave the aid we
    sought,
To deck our halls their gems of art have sent,
Or deign'd to grace our peaceful tournament,

Where Labour's toiling ranks, in bloodless fray,
With friendly rivalry their skill display.

See where on either side their trophies stand,
The high-wrought triumphs of the skilful hand
Whose perfect handicraft, in every part,
Reveals the well-trained workman's finished art,
And by their massive strength we may compare
The fragile beauties wrought by fingers fair,
Like bright-hued flow'rets in the forest glade
Nestling beneath some giant gum-tree's shade.

We pray you next, with kindly glance survey
The crowning triumph of our youth to-day,
Where young Ambition, panting for a prize,
Shows his achievements to our wond'ring eyes,
And in the youthful effort plain appears
The promised excellence of riper years,
As orchard-blossoms in the verdant Spring
Foretell the fruits the golden Autumns bring.

Fain would we linger, 'midst a scene so fair,
To scan each object, view each beauty rare,
Proclaim the triumph of the sons of Toil,
And praise each trophy of the teeming soil,
Point to the wond'rous things our lads have
        made,
Portray the matchless skill of each fair maid,

And tell how friends, in many a distant town
Their aid have lent, our enterprise to crown.

But at the board where guests expectant throng,
Keen Hunger wearies at a grace too long.
'Tis time the Poet should lay down the lyre,
The song should cease ere patient list'ners tire.
One last sweet note we'd sound, full loud and
    clear,
A note to wake the echoes far and near,
A note to rise in accents clear and strong,
A note of welcome—Welcome to Geelong!

EPILOGUE

Spoken at the close of the Geelong Exhibition

WHEN, at the close of some long Summer's
    day,
The westering sun sinks o'er Corio's Bay,
When flaming robes the distant hills enfold,
And skies are radiant with reflected gold,
When dawn's bright hues the dark'ning
    heavens adorn,
And fading day assumes the garb of morn—
We scarce can credit that a scene so bright
Should be but herald of the gloomy night.

With equal wonder now our eyes survey
This fair assembly and this bright array;
No trace is seen, in this glad festive hour,
Of fell decay, to prove Time's fatal power.
No twilight gloom, no gathering clouds reveal
The final hour our hearts alone may feel;
This closing scene reflects in tints so gay,
The festal glories of our opening day.

So would we have it, and His name we bless
Who crowns our efforts with this large success,
Who decks our face with smiles, our path with
     flowers,
And sends this joy to grace our closing hours.
With Him we leave our work, and humbly
     pray,
Let not its influence quickly pass away;
May coming years in rich profusion show
Full bounteous harvests from the seed we
     sow.

Fain would we hope that in the years beyond
Shall richer fruitage to our toil respond,
Success achieved dispels our former fears,
And glad expectancy awaits the years
When youthful hands, that emulous here have
     wrought,

Have gained the skill by long experience
    bought,
And they whose feet here first essayed to climb,
Have reached of Fame's bright mount the
    heights sublime.

Thus, like the evening star that decks the sky,
Ere sunset glories, gently fading, die,
Bright Hope beams forth, and 'neath its
    tranquil spell,
Our hearts would softly breathe one word—
    " Farewell ;"
Farewell—that word brings now no thought
    of pain,
But echoes lightly like some sweet refrain ;
For though we part, 'tis not as on the shore
Sad friends are parted who shall meet no
    more.

Full oft, we trust, in coming days, these halls
Shall woo our feet within their sheltering walls ;
Short be the night, and bright the coming morn
When fresh attraction shall our courts adorn.
Long may they stand to grace our fair Geelong,
The haunts of beauty and the home of song ;
And like success each faithful effort crown,
That seeks the welfare of Corio's town.

INAUGURAL POEM

FOR THE JUBILEE TEMPERANCE CONVENTION

*Held during the currency of the Adelaide International
Exhibition, 1887*

The voice of joy in a Southern Land ;
    A song o'er the sunlit sea !
There are dancing feet on the golden strand,
    And a shout of Jubilee,
For the nations have come from far to greet
    A sister land sweet and fair,
They have come to lay at her busy feet
    Their gifts and trophies rare.

Gather, O friends of our Southern Land,
    And warm shall your welcome be,
We will joyfully grasp each outstretch'd hand
    In our hour of Jubilee !
And a place shall be yours in joyous song,
    A place in the home of prayer ;
Each joy that is ours to you shall belong
    And you shall our glories share.

"We bring a gift for this Southern Land,
    A treasure from o'er the sea;
A blessing of peace for each toiling hand
    In this year of Jubilee."
What boon have ye brought from your distant
       shores,
    What pledge from your hearts of flame?
What wealth do you lay at our open doors,
    In our dawning hour of fame?

"We bring in love to this Southern Land,
    A prayer that shall make it free;
With the earnest heart and the helping hand
    In its day of Jubilee;
That the thraldom of drink may pass away
    From altar and home and store,
And Temperance reign with its peaceful sway
    In its borders evermore.

"That a light may shine in this Southern Land
    And flame o'er the glittering sea;
While they dance and sing on the golden strand
    With the shout of Jubilee.
That the news may fly, by a seraph borne,
    With joy to the Courts above;
That each weary chain by the drunkard worn
    Is burst by the power of Love."

CHILDREN'S VOICES

Hark, hark! for children's voices
Are singing loud and clear,
And every heart rejoices
The children's song to hear.
    They sing of homes made gladsome,
    Of gardens bright with flowers,
    Of glorious work for Temp'rance done,
    In this fair land of ours.

They sing of hearts uniting,
Through life to bravely stand,
The cause of Temp'rance fighting,
In this fair southern land.
    They sing of lives made happy,
    Of Wisdom's large increase—
    The harvest rich of kindly words,
    Of purity and peace.

They sing of young lives guarded
From Drink's destructive power—
Of holy laws regarded,
In childhood's sunlit hour.
    They sing the joyous present,
    Of future happy days,
    Of lives in paths of safety spent—
    To God eternal praise.

CHRISTMAS EVE AT FERNSHAW

A REMINISCENCE

I

WHERE the dusky grove of myrtle
  Casts a shadow, deep and drear:
Where, 'midst mossy banks enshrouded,
  Hides the streamlet, bright and clear:
Where the Fern-king holds his revels
  In his hidden courts of green,
And the wire-grass weaves a curtain
  To enshrine the mystic scene:

II

There I lingered, in the gloaming
  Of a sunny Christmastide;
There I lingered 'midst the shadows,
  While the daylight waned and died;
There I mused and dreamed and pondered
  Of the happy days of yore,
Ere my errant feet had wandered
  To this strange Australian shore.

III

O'er me swayed a leafy curtain
  Of clematis, wild and sweet,
Mossy cushions, soft and silent,
  Coyly clasped my ling'ring feet;
Pendulous creepers swung beside me,
  Fluttering leaves around me played,
Gently dancing to the music
  By the wand'ring zephyrs made.

IV

High above me, gently swaying
  As the light breeze wandered by,
Mighty monarchs of the forest
  Waved their branches to the sky:
Tall, and straight, and bare, their columns
  Caught the sunset's fading beam,
Till their gold was turned to silver
  In the moonlight's paler gleam.

V

Sweeter than the perfumed incense,
  Swung from censers, rich and rare,
Forest odours, sweet and fragrant,
  Floated on the balmy air;
While, a deeper silence hushing
  All except the streamlet's cry,
Faded out the last faint flushing
  From the slowly dark'ning sky.

VI

Soft and still the evening gathered,
  Closed me round with curtains grey,
Curtains grey of pearly radiance,
  Glinting in the moon's pale ray.
Gleamed the fern fronds slowly waving;
  Gleamed the light mists o'er the vale:
Gleamed each silv'ry leaf, whose rustling
  Mark'd the gently passing gale.

VII

In that hour, my spirit weary
  Restful grew. All soothed and calm,
Fell the beauty and the silence
  On my wounded heart like balm;
Hopes, long buried, rose within me,
  Joys, long vanished, cheered once more,
Mem'ry fond drew brightest pictures
  Of a loved, though distant, shore.

VIII

Flew my soul, on wings of fancy,
  Far across the rolling main,
And in thought I wandered gaily
  'Midst familiar scenes again.
Plain I saw the dear old homestead,
  Gabled, thatched, and diamond paned,
Where, enthroned 'midst sweet contentment,
  Peace and love together reigned.

IX

Rose the fair old home before me
  Where my boyhood passed away,
Rose the dear old friends around me,
  Dear old faces, gone for aye.
Voices hushed seemed sounding near me,
  Loving voices, sweet and low,
Whisp'ring of a love that cheered me,
  Of a Christmas long ago.

X

All the old familar landscape
  In its winter garb of snow
Glittered in the frosty starlight
  And the casement's warmer glow.
There the pond where oft I'd skated,
  There the gate where oft I'd swung,
In the days when life was golden,
  In the days when I was young.

XI

Glowed my heart with fond emotion,
  Dreaming thus of days gone by,
But the bright illusion vanished
  As the night-bird's mournful cry
Sounded through the lonely forest,
  While afar I heard the fall,
Crashing loudly through the ranges,
  Of some sylvan vet'ran tall.

XII

Sadly now, amidst the branches
  Wailed the breeze, with fitful sighs;
Sadly gleamed the stars above me,
  Shining down with pitying eyes,
O'er me fell a cloud of sadness,
  Sank my heart with trembling fears,
And the woe of joys departed
  Touched the secret fount of tears.

XIII

But, as though my grief to solace,
  Through the stillness, soft and low,
Comes the sweet clear voice of children
  From the school-house far below;
Through the woods the echoes sounded,
  On my heart the message fell
Of the sweet old Christmas story,
  Which those voices rose to tell.

XIV

Rising like the sweet old carols
  Sung of yore amidst the snow,
Rising like the midnight music
  Heard in childhood, long ago,
When the notes to which we listened,
  With their soft mysterious strains,
Seemed an echo of the anthem
  Angels sang o'er Judah's plains.

53

THE CHILDREN'S CHRISTMAS HYMN

Sing we to the Lord of glory,
  Christ we hail with hymns of praise,
When our hearts would tell the story
  Of the good that crowns our days.
May we in His glad creation,
  In the wonders of His grace,
View the Lord of our Salvation,
  See the brightness of His face.

Morning star, o'er Bethlehem shining,
  Guide us to His lowly bed;
Evening lights, at day's declining,
  Soft reveal His weary head;
Flowers that bloom 'midst thorn and briar,
  Shadow forth His footsteps fair:
Birds' sweet song, in tuneful choir,
  Sing His love and guardian care.

Lives of those, the pure and holy,
  Who His gentle sway confess,
Who, in stations high or lowly,
  Seek, like Him, the world to bless;
Deeds of mercy, love, and duty,
  Humble worth, or noble fame,
Whisper to our hearts the beauty
  Of our blest Redeemer's name.

Thus the Christ Emanuel viewing
  In the good His saints have done,
May we, in their steps pursuing,
  Follow till our course be run.
Follow till His arms receive us
  In His mansions fair, above,
Where no sin nor toil shall grieve us,
  Resting in His boundless love.

XV

Sank the voices into silence,
  Ceased the music, sweet, and clear,
But the song had soothed my sorrow,
  And its message chased my fear;
Banished were my sad forebodings,
  Vanished every thought of care—
To my spirit, soft, caressing,
  Came the holy calm of prayer.

SOUL WINGS

(A TRANSLATION FROM THE FRENCH.)

WHAT though thy path through life be bare,
  And sorrow be thy dole!
Though earth's foundations sink in air,
  Hast thou not still thy soul?

Hath it not wings to bear thee up,
  Where purer winds have blown,
Above, beyond, the world's sad cry,
  The murmur and the groan?

Be like the bird that lightly sways
  The branch on which he sings;
'Tis frail, yet he his song ne'er stays,
  He knows that he has wings.

THE COMING MEN

I

FROM the misty caves of the by-gone years,
  The shades of the long ago,
Come echoes of laughter and flashings of tears,
  The voices of mirth and woe.
There were joys and sorrows and hopes and
      fears,
  The victor, the vanquished, then,
But, watchman, what of the coming years?
  And what of the coming men?

II

'Midst the shadows deep of these cloud-wrapt
      days,
  We plod in the vales below,
Yet upward we glance to the heralding rays,
  That gleam on the hills aglow.

While far in the distance the traveller hears,
  As he struggles through swamp and fen,
The chariot wheels of the coming years,
  The march of the coming men.

III

Do we idly dream of that fairer dawn,
  More bright than the world has known,
When the curtains of night are at last with-
      drawn,
  And the twilight stars have flown?
Do we watch in vain for the light that nears
  The glorious noontide then,
To brighten the days of the coming years,
  And shine o'er the coming men?

IV

When vanished away is this century old,
  And passed like a burning scroll,
What wonders undreamt of may then unfold
  And burst on each dazzled soul;
For the seeker shall find the truth that cheers,
  And knowledge shall guide the pen,
If the sword be sheathed in the coming years,
  And peace rule the coming men.

V

When they surely know, where we feebly
      guessed,
  And stand where we ne'er could climb,

When, passing each mark towards which we
    have pressed,
They traverse those heights sublime,
Will they scorn our labours, or mock our fears
    In pride, or in pity, then,
In the clearer light of the coming years,
    The strength of the coming men?

VI

No matter. Be ours to level the road,
    Removing each barrier stone,
For to every heart is its destined load,
    And we live not for time alone.
We will plough in hope, or we'll sow in tears,
    For the joyful reaping then,
Though our names be lost in the coming years,
    Nor heard by the coming men.

LINES

SUGGESTED BY THE EXHIBITION OF MR. WOOD-
ROFFE'S GLASS STEAM ENGINE

I WANDERED forth, in labour's busy hour,
And saw, on ev'ry hand, steam's mighty power.
I saw the monster panting by the mine,
Or flying madly o'er the metalled line;
I watched it urging from our peaceful shore
Full freighted ships the stormy ocean o'er;

Or, in the factory, 'midst whirring bands,
Perform with ease the work of myriad hands.

I wandered on, till I beheld at last
A spot o'er which its mighty wrath had past—
A scene appalling, massive walls were rent,
And iron bars, like straws, were torn and bent ;
Great beams lay splintered, mighty stones up-
turned.
Huge columns shattered—where the fires had
burned,
Blackness and darkness.   Then, in fear, I cried
" No power so vast is found on earth beside."

That night in Woodroffe's hall, with wond'ring
eyes,
I saw this power in strangely different guise,
Curbed with a crystal chain, and held with bands
That scarce had borne the shock of infant
hands ;
(So the proud steed that spurned the desert
plain
Is trained obedient to my lady's rein.)
Mild as the lamb that, garlanded with flowers,
Sports wi' the bairns in Spring's soft, sunny
hours.

I saw the giant steam, a Samson bound,
Compelled to turn a tiny mill-wheel round,

While glittering wheels revolved the stampers
    fell
With tinkling music, like a fairy's bell ;
High in the air the jetting fountain threw
The crystal drops that fell again like dew.

A fairy vision! Such, I thought the while,
Do white-souled children dream and sleeping
    smile.
I learned this lesson, in that evening hour,
That mightier far than steam's tremendous
    power,
Is that which lurks within the human will,
The power of intellect and well-trained skill.

THE MESSAGE OF THE SWAN

TO A YOUNG LADY ON HER WEDDING MORN
(WITH THE GIFT OF A CRYSTAL SWAN)

As glides the swan across the lake's deep calm,
With mien unruffled and secure from harm,
She sees reflected in her glassy home
The shining semblance of the azure dome:

Two kindred joys for thee a friend would crave:
A placid journey o'er life's gleaming wave,
And in thy home, illumed by peace and love,
A bright reflection of the heaven above.

AT EVENTIDE

When the evening shades are falling,
  On the night breeze, soft and low,
Come sweet voices, oft recalling,
  Treasured joys of long ago.

Whispering voices, 'midst the hushing,
  Shadowy faces, 'midst the gloom,
Gleams of long past sunsets, flushing
  Golden beams o'er many a tomb.

Kisses warm, from lips long frozen,
  Loving tones, of voices gone,
Salvage rare, from Death's dark ocean,
  Borne by waves of memory on.

Soft the sighs that rise unbidden,
  While the evening shadows fall,
Sweet the tears that rise unchidden,
  When our hearts the past recall.

THE ORANGE LILY IN AUSTRALIA

A PLANT from Ulster's soil I drew
    And bore it o'er the sea ;
Beside my southern home it grew,
    A treasure there to me.
It blooms beneath our clearer skies
    As in old Erin's glades ;
As fair where Yarra's waters rise
    As 'neath Knockmany's* shade.

Just as of old I watched it bloom
    Amidst the emerald hills,
And saw it gleam in twilight gloom
    Beside the murmuring rills,
I see it blossom bright and fair
    Beneath the Austral sky,
Its leaves as green, its hue as rare,
    Its form as straight and high.

It wears the glowing tints of dawn,
    It mocks the sunset's ray,
It bears the glories of the morn
    Through the long summer day ;
Its bloom repays my willing toil,
    I smiled to find it grew

*Knockmany, a well-known h   in County Tyrone.

As freely in our virgin soil
  As in the land it knew.

And shall the flower bloom alone
  Or blossom all in vain ?
Brings it no word our sires have known
  Across the heaving main ?
Hath it no mem'ries brave enwrought
  Within its breast of gold ?
Have we no hearts, by wisdom taught,
  Its message to unfold ?

Blooming beneath an alien sky
  As in its home of yore,
Holding its head as fair and high
  As on its native shore,
" Unchanged in all but place," in dreams
  It whispers unto me ;
" Unchanged in all but place" it seems
  Our duty here to be.

To hold the faith our fathers held,
  To keep the truths they knew,
To bar each wrong their lives repelled
  With hearts as firm and true,
To plant the flag they bravely bore
  Beside the southern sea,
And wear upon this new found shore
  The colours of the free.

"NOT AS THOSE WITHOUT HOPE"

Call them not dead who pass from earth's
dark dwelling
To live in mansions of celestial light,
Where joys are found all earthly bliss excelling,
And purblind Faith gives place to perfect sight.

Not dead : each well-remembered voice is
singing
Songs of sweet import at our open door ;
The music of their footsteps still is ringing
Around the thresholds they may cross no
more.

Not dead: though, slipping from our fond
embraces,
They spread their wings and soar to worlds
above ;
Their shining course our eye with rapture traces,
Beyond our arms, but not beyond our love.

Not they, the dead, but we, who in the
gloaming,
Grope 'midst the shadows of earth's murky
night ;
Nor life we know, till, with our dear ones
roaming,
We tread the pathways of Eternal Light.

PROLOGUE

FOR " YE OLDE ENGLISH FAYRE," HELD AT
BALLARAT IN THE YEAR 1882.

DREAMS within dreams! The future frames the
    past!
Pale dawnlight rays flit o'er our noonday
    skies!
An old-world revel greets our wond'ring gaze,
    And mocks our senses with a glad surprise.

Here, 'midst such scenes as olden poets
    dreamed,
Of golden cities in a sunlit land,
Where freedom dances and where plenty reigns,
    And boundless fortune fills the toiler's hand :

We mirror back the lights of days long fled,
    The ancient pastimes and the quaint old
    ways,
The garb and manners of a long past age,
    The " Merrie England" of the olden days.

Thus, though Time backward never turns his
    glass,
    Though days, once vanished, may return no
    more,
We show our children how our fathers lived,
    And took their pleasure in the days of yore.

And thus we strive, though distant shores we
    tread,
Though alien stars shine o'er us from above,
Around the thresholds of our new found homes,
    To plant sweet mem'ries of a land we love.

Then look not harshly on this mimic scene,
    Scan not our revels with the critic's eye,
But let kind fancy gently lull each sense,
    With pleasant visions of the days gone by.

VERSE

WRITTEN TO BE PLACED IN CABINET CONTAINING
SOME SHELLS SENT FROM MALDEN ISLAND

ONLY some shells that strew'd a distant strand,
    On lonely shores by careless billows hurled,
Yet each the impress bears of that great Hand
    Which decks with beauty all the radiant
    world.

IN MEMORIAM

HENRY KENDALL.

Oh! there is silence in the forest now:
The tender leaves hang motionless,
Or, with a noiseless quiver, as in pain,
Tremble and droop and fall.
                    But yesterday
A singer filled these glades with melody;
These lichens and these mosses were his books
Wherein he learned strange harmonies!
These winds that sob and moan—when he
          was by
Sang weird and mystic songs, which he alone
Might hear and understand. These glinting lights
That struggle through the branches, traced
Upon the ground strange characters
Which only he might read!
These sullen forest dells revealed to him
Their mysteries of wonder; he communed
With nature and with beauty till his heart,
Too full for silence, burst in song.
                    Alas! too few
Have cared to listen to the tuneful voice—
Yet he sang on, for God appointed him
To be a singer in this morning land.
                    His harp lies shattered now—
Silent and broken! It is fit that we
Should weep in silence, for we have no voice
As sweet as his to sing his elegy—
          " Kendall is dead."

A NUPTIAL WISH

WRITTEN DURING A VISIT TO SCOTLAND, AND
ADDRESSED TO MISS WALKER, OF INVER-
NESS, ON THE OCCASION OF HER MARRIAGE.

WARM as the winds that fan my southern
home,
Pure as the moonlight's beam, the sea's white
foam,
The wish I send—
That fortune's hand thy northern home may
build,
That all sweet joys thy nuptial hours may gild,
Fair, new found friend.

Oft, as across the distant seas I fly,
Or where the Southern Cross adorns the sky,
My thoughts will trace
The pleasant paths the Ness's shore that bound
The rich, abundant pastures that surround
Thy native place.

That thou in pleasant paths may still be led,
With rich abundance round thy footsteps
spread,
My heart shall pray
That earth's best blessings all thy life may grace
Till time's soft twilight shall at last give place
To endless day.

"THERE SHALL BE NO MORE SEA"

(An unfinished poem)

"There shall be no more sea!" Round Pat-
    mos' isle
The gloomy waters surging swept, the while
The loved apostle, aged, and alone,
Gazed o'er its depths, and heard its sullen tone.

Then thunder's mighty voice, with menace
    dire,
Shook the reverb'rant skies, with baleful fire
Illuminate; the solid rocks around
Reel 'midst the concourse of tremendous sound.

With thund'rous shock the waves invade the
    shore,
Round the frail cot tempestuous horrors roar,
But all the terrors that their souls assail
Are for the absent ones who face the gale.

"There shall be no more sea!" Upon that
    shore
No stormy waves impinge, no tempests roar,
But parting clouds shall placid skies disclose,
And peaceful stars look down in soft repose.

Never again the wrestling winds shall bear
Above their din, the voice of hoarse despair,
Nor e'er again shall rend the sullen sky
Fear's frantic shrick, or death's appalling cry.

No stalwart ship with sudden shock shall reel,
No treach'rous rock shall rive the fateful keel,
And never more the angry waves shall lay
Upon the oozy strand their lifeless prey.

No wretch forlorn shall pace the dark'ning
strand
With anxious gaze, or point with trembling
hand,
Shall watch with fearful eyes the rising gale,
Or hopeless wait the unreturning sail.

Ne'er through the gloom profound of murky
night,
The cottage pane shall cast its wistful light,
Where tearful watchers wait, of hope forlorn,
The dread revealings of the threat'ning morn.

No quivering lip shall speak the sad farewell,
No tortured heart with parting anguish swell,
No teardrop hide the swift receding shore,
When friends are sundered who shall meet
no more.

VICTORIA'S SONG OF PRAISE

QUEEN VICTORIA'S DIAMOND JUBILEE, 1897

WHERE'ER a British flag shall wave
 O'er sea or shore to-day,
Where'er a British heart shall beat,
 Or British voices pray,
One thought alone each soul inspires,
 Though oceans roll between,
One impulse tunes each willing heart
 In homage to our Queen.

One song upon the northern blast
 Rides with a trumpet tone,
It echoes on from shore to shore,
 And sounds from zone to zone;
Across the startled world it rings,
 Where'er our flag is seen,
The theme the mighty anthem bears
 Is homage to our Queen.

Here in the land that bears her name,
 Born 'neath her sovereign sway,
We, children of the sunny south,
 Join in that song to-day.
We joy to think how long her reign,
 How bright its fame has been,
And high our festal voices raise
 In homage to our Queen.

71

Thus with her people far and near
    With joined hands we sing,
And send the glowing anthem on,
    Around the world to ring.
One thought alone each soul inspires,
    Though oceans roll between,
One impulse tunes each willing heart
    In homage to our Queen.

HOMAGE TO OUR QUEEN

VICTORIAN DIAMOND JUBILEE HYMN

Tune—" Men of Harlech"

(Sung at the Exhibition Building, Melbourne, on 25th
June, 1897, by 17,000 Sunday-school children.)

Hark! A mighty empire singing!
Round the globe the song is ringing,
On the air this cadence flinging,
        Homage to our Queen!
Nations young and nations hoary
Rise to tell Victoria's story,
Sing her radiant reign of glory,
        Homage to our Queen!
    Take the swelling chorus,
    South wind breathing o'er us,
        Bear the strain
        Across the main,

72

    Bear this loving greeting
From the land her name enshrining,
Where the starry cross is shining,
And where southern flowers are twining,
      Bear it to our Queen.

Shores which austral seas are laving,
Proudly see her banners waving,
Love alone our hearts enslaving,
      Homage to our Queen!
Firm her throne on right is grounded,
Safe, by loyal hearts surrounded,
On a people's love 'tis founded,
      Homage to our Queen!
    Take the swelling chorus
    South wind breathing o'er us,
      Bear the strain
      Across the main,
    Bear Victoria's greeting,
Long may love and peace attend her,
From all ill may Heaven defend her,
Added length of days still send her,
      Long o'er us to reign.

AUSTRALIA

A FEDERATION HYMN

(The last verses written by J. W. Meaden.)

LAND of the south, where freedom dwells
 Beneath a cloudless sky,
Where guardian seas in pride reflect
 The starry cross on high.
  Thy sons renew their vows this day
   To guard thy shores from ill,
  And keep thee through the years to be
   The home of freedom still.

Land of the south, where plenty deigns
 To bless the fruitful soil,
And smiling hope eternal reigns
 To cheer the sons of toil.
  Thy people's love shall serve thee well
   In danger's threat'ning hour,
  Their loyal hearts thy bulwark strong
   Against oppression's power.

God of the universe, we pray,
 Bless Thou our southern land,
And guard, till time's remotest day,
 Our fair Australian strand.
  And whilst its children bend the knee,
   Obedient to Thy will,
  Keep Thou our coasts that they may be
   The home of freedom still.

THE ARGONAUTS

A CANTATA

ARGUMENT

THE DEPARTURE.—(1) The Rest of the Golden Fleece in the sacred Grove of Ares. (2) Rumour conveys abroad the fame thereof, and paints glowing pictures of the beauties of the western lands, the Garden of the Hesperides, &c.; adding a gentle warning against the allurements of the Sirens, who, standing upon the shore, seek by their songs to entice the mariners to destruction. (3) Attracted by these reports, the Argonautic heroes set forth on their adventurous voyage. Labouring at the oars, they sing with joyful hearts, and commit themselves, alike in storm and sunshine, to the protection of the Sea-god.

THE RETURN.—(1) After a lengthened absence, during which many dangers and hardships have been experienced, the Argonauts, returning in triumph with the Golden Fleece, once more behold the walls of their beloved Iolcos, lapped by the sparkling waters of the Pagasæan Gulf. (2) Reaching the shore, they are met by bands of maidens, who, with singing and dancing, conduct them to the gate of the City. (3) Here their countrymen receive them with songs of triumphant welcome, amidst which they proceed to the Temple of Neptune, where, with sacrificial rites, they deposit the Golden Fleece, and dedicate their vessel, the *Argo*, to the Sea-god, who, accepting the offering, raises it to the skies, there to shine as a constellation for the guidance of mariners. (4) Elated by their reception, the Argonauts joyfully redeem the vows made during their absence, upon the whole assemblage join in a solemn invocation to Neptune.

NOTE BY THE AUTHOR.—As in this instance the ordinary routine of composition has been reversed (the labour of the composer having preceded that of the writer), the latter has been compelled to act in a somewhat arbitrary manner, both in his selection of the incidents to be illustrated and his method of treating them. For this reason, also, the circumstances attending the actual discovery of the Golden Fleece are omitted, and the entire story reduced within the slenderest limits. For the sake of unity, the scene of the consecration of the Argo, traditionally located in the Isthmus of Corinth, is transferred to Iolcos.—J.W.M.

PART I.—THE DEPARTURE

INTRODUCTION

RECITATIVE—BASS

On distant shores, in solitude profound,
Where mystic shades the sylvan shrine sur-
    round;
In sacred groves of deep and solemn gloom,
Where baleful stars predict th' intruder's
    doom—
    By monsters guarded, and by magic spell—
    The Golden Fleece illumes the silent dell.

CHORUS

Come sail o'er seas of pleasure,
    Where dark'ning skies ne'er frown,
To seek this regal treasure,
    This prize of high renown.
        Beyond the shadows olden
            That guard the unknown west,
        In the regions bright and golden
            Where the red sun sinks to rest.

There fruits of golden lustre
    Between the branches shine,
And grapes in purple cluster
    Hang drooping from the vine.

There fair-brow'd maids lie dreaming
In bowers of blissful ease ;
And resplendent cities, gleaming
Through the haze of golden seas.

Come, sail o'er glitt'ring waters,
By gentle zephyrs fann'd ;
While beauty's fairest daughters
Stand beck'ning on the strand,
Their songs, like sweet bells ringing,
Float soft on the balmy air ;
Fair and false so sweetly singing,
O wanderer, then beware !

THE HEROES' SONG

(Chorus of Male Voices.)

Now bend we to the lab'ring oar,
That cleaves the glassy wave ;
With haste we flee th' enchanted shore,
The treacherous mermaid's cave.
No luring joy our course shall stay,
No threatening danger bar our way.

Though angry tempests round us roar,
And Jove's loud thunders crash ;
Though whirling torrents round us pour,
And the salt spray o'er us dash ;
Our course to stay they strive in vain,
For the Sea-god rules o'er the heaving main.

PART II—THE RETURN

Pastorale

RECITATIVE—TENOR

Once more, 'mid pastures fair and verdant
groves enshrined,
The sun-lit seas before, the purple hills behind ;
Guarded by frowning forts where watchful
sentries stand,
By Neptune's sacred shrine, and vestured
priestly band ;
The scene of home beloved now cheers
each warrior's sight,
Iolcos stands in view, all bathed in rosy
light.

CHORUS OF MAIDENS

Now to the shore, a joyful train,
We gaily haste with dancing feet ;
While loud we chant a glad refrain,
With smiles the warrior band to greet,
Bearing the Golden Fleece.

CHORAL SONG OF WELCOME

All hail ! ye sons of glory, through ev'ry age
and clime
Your names shall live in story, embalm'd by
deeds sublime ;

Your brows with wreaths undying, immortal
shall be crown'd,
And Fame, on swift wing flying, your praises
shall resound.

We welcome you with singing, we greet you
at the shore,
The sacred chalice bringing, we glad libations
pour ;
While votive floods are streaming, and costly
victims slain,
The Golden Fleece shall, gleaming, adorn the
Sea-god's fane.

Now at thy sacred altar,
Neptune, on thee we call ;
With tongues that ne'er may falter,
To thee we give our all :
That thine by consecration
The Argo hence may be,
A shining constellation,
A light for those at sea.

SOLO, QUARTETT, AND CHORUS

THE INVOCATION

Great Neptune, ruler of the foaming wave,
Whose mighty hand with trembling smites
the world ;

By whose stern voice the howling winds are
    roused,
And stubborn mountains from their bases
    hurl'd.

To hear us, check thy rapid courser's flight,
And let thy car's swift rolling wheels be stayed;
Behold our offerings borne across the wave,
Accept the gifts upon thine altars laid.

TO MY NIECE

ON HER WEDDING DAY

A BLESSING on thy home, through all the years,
'Midst joys and sorrows and through smiles
    and tears,
In Summer sunshine and through wintry
    weather,
For man must take the rough and smooth
    together.

May Hope's bright lamp illume thy darkest
    hours,
And sorrows pass like Spring's light fleeting
    showers ;
By lasting comfort may thy health be blest,
And fair contentment make thy cot its nest.

THE CHILDREN'S GIFTS

THE children sat in the ingle nook,
  For the night, out doors, was chill,
The fierce rain beat on the window pane,
  And the winds blew wild and shrill;
But the bairns were safe in the warm home nest,
  Sweet lambs within the fold,
And the firelight flash'd in their sparkling eyes
  And their clustering curls of gold.

White robed and fair, in the glancing light,
  Demure and quiet they sat,
But each little ear was open wide
  To list to the old folks' chat,
And the old folks talked of each plan so wise
  And the wondrous things they'd made
" For the sake of the Church we love so well,
  And the dear Lord's sake," they said.

The children listened with faces wise,
  And talked in whispers low
Of each holy child who serv'd the Lord
  In the ages long ago;
Of Samuel, clad in his little coat,
  Op'ning the temple door;
Of the Hebrew youths who stood unhurt
  On the fiery furnace floor.

How the dear child Christ in His Father's
    house
'Midst the doctors wise had stood ;
How Jesus had blest the babes of old
    As only the Saviour could.
And can we do nought, was the thought, I ween,
    That came to each wee, wise head,
" For the sake of the Church we love so well,
    For the dear Lord's sake," they said.

The old folks fell into silence then,
    To list to the children's voice,
And the artless plans which they heard unfold
    Made their own warm hearts rejoice.
When they heard how wisely each young voice
    spake,
    How wisely each young head plann'd,
How each young heart longed to the Lord to
    bring
    The work of a child's weak hand.

The old folks listened, and think ye not
    That the dear Lord listened too?
And think ye not He will bless each gift
    From a young heart, fond and true.
Each gift that a loving heart has plann'd,
    Or a willing hand has made?
" For the sake of the Church we love so well,
    For the dear Lord's sake," they said.

YOUTHFUL TOILERS

A CANTATA

*Specially written for the Sunday School Industrial Exhibition,
October, 1896.*

INVOCATION—(CHORUS)

O GOD, who made the Sabbath day
  And hallowed it as Thine,
Teach us to prize with rev'rent care
  That gift of grace divine.
May we with thoughts of His great love
  Its blissful hours employ,
Who gave it to His toiling sons
  That they might share its joy.
We share Thy Sabbath rest, O Lord,
  Bless Thou our days of toil,
Accept the gifts our hands have wrought,
  Or nurtured from the soil.

SWEET SABBATH BELLS—(CHORUS)

When sounds the peaceful Sabbath chime,
  And man from toil a while may rest,
We open wide the Book sublime,
  And find each sacred hour is blest.
          Ring on, sweet Sabbath bells,
          Sweet Sabbath bells, ring on!

And through each workday's busy hours,
  Amidst our labour and our play,

83

Come, sweet as scent of op'ning flowers,
Glad mem'ries of that holy day.
Ring on, sweet Sabbath bells,
Sweet Sabbath bells, ring on!

So through each year that swiftly rolls,
Until our earthly course be o'er,
May holy teachings guide our souls
In peace to Heaven's fair restful shore.
Ring on, sweet Sabbath bells,
Sweet Sabbath bells, ring on!

THE PROMISE OF CHILDHOOD

DUET—SOPRANO AND TENOR

Long ere the bright-hued perfumed flowers
May summer glories bring,
In tender grace come stealing forth
The early buds of spring.

Before the autumn's golden sheaves
May crown the fruitful year,
In modest robe of emerald clad
The tiny blades appear.

And ere the finished work be wrought,
Befitting manhood's prime,
The promise comes in well spent hours
Of childhood's earliest time.

The Merry Anvil—(chorus)

The merry anvil ringing
  Awakes the dewy morn,
And mocks the hammer swinging
  By youthful workers borne ;
While on the breeze come blending
  The sounds of cheerful toil,
And songs of children tending
  The trophies of the soil.

They sing in morning gladness,
  Their hearts with joy aglow,
Earth's burdens and its sadness
  Not yet their lives may know ;
And still the sounds of labour
  With children's voices blend,
While youthful toilers gather
  To praise their Heavenly Friend.

Evil Stands Ever Near—(chorus)

Evil stands ever near, luring our gaze !
Guide Thou our wayward feet into Thy ways.
Teach us in tenderness still to pursue
Life's narrow upward road, steadfast and true.
Toiler of Nazareth, list to our prayer,
Lead us in wisdom's ways—pleasant and fair.

85

Thou Who in Childhood's Lowly Guise

SOPRANO—SOLO AND CHORUS

Thou, who in childhood's lowly guise
Disdained not lowly toil,
And loved the fragrant flowers that bloomed
On Canaan's fruitful soil.

Who took the children in Thine arms,
And blessed them as they came,
Bless Thou the children of our land
Who gather in Thy name.

Bless Thou the work of youthful hands,
The flowers they fondly tend,
Guide Thou their steps in righteous paths,
Their Guardian and their Friend.

Now Our Cheerful Voices Blending

FINAL CHORUS AND FUGUE

Now our cheerful voices blending,
Loud the triune God we praise,
Who, with mercies never ending,
Crowns with joy our youthful days.

Praise we sing to God the Father,
Power ascribe to God the Son,
Glory give to God the Spirit,
Glory give the Three in One.

AUSTRALIA

A CANTATA POEM

I

Awake, O Southern Harp !
Too long with chords unstrung
Above these fertile plains
In silence hung.
Sing, sing ! ye daughters of this sunny land ;
Rejoice ! my brothers on the Austral strand ;
Hail this triumphal morn with joyful lays,
A hundred years of light demands our praise.

A SONG OF THE PAST

Softly the leaves in the woodland fell
Where the fern fronds waved in the mossy dell,
And softly sang, like a murmuring shell,
The surf on the long, low shore.

No ship's white wing flecked the purple seas,
And the loudest note on the summer breeze
Was the bell-bird's call 'midst the forest trees,
Ere the sultry day was o'er.

But nightly the camp-fires flickering low,
Through the branches gleamed with a fitful glow,
Where the wild man watched for his lurking foe,
    In the silent years of yore.

II

Sing of the fateful dawn when first a meteor
    flag unfurled,
And Britain's empire glories gleamed above a
    new-found world ;
When, in the shades where silence dwelt, a
    voice was heard at last
That banished from these golden lands the
    shadows of the past.

A SONG OF LABOUR

Then Labour leaped upon the strand,
    " Ho !" merrily laughed he,
And beckoned with his brawny hand
    To those across the sea.
" Ye toiling hands from older lands,
    O hither make your way ;
This new-found shore hath plenteous store
    My vot'ries to repay.

" We'll build fair cities where alone
    The dusky savage crept,
And Commerce shall erect her throne
    Where wild birds nightly slept ;

The harvest swains the lonely plains
  Shall cheer with dance and song,
While teeming wealth and jocund health
  Enrich the lab'ring throng."

III

Your festal songs, O friends, a moment stay,
Let pensive thoughts your tender bosoms sway;
These grassy mounds around demand a tear,
Bedeck with flowers this day each hero's bier.

A SONG OF THE PIONEERS

They were worthy sons of the Norsemen old,
  And their land was fair and free,
But their ships were stout and their hearts
      were bold,
  So they steered for the unknown sea;
And a flag they bore that of glory told,
  As they sailed o'er the southern sea.
Their arms were as strong as their hearts
      were bold,
  So they felled the forest tree,
And they built their homes in the land of gold
  Which they found o'er the unknown sea,
And the flag unfurled that of glory told,
  On the shores of the southern sea.

IV

Now let our infant empire's strength
Inspire a useful strain,
To tell how new-born nations dwell
Beside the southern main ;
A century of progress, a hundred years of toil
Have wrought a wondrous harvest on the
fruitful Austral soil.

The trophies of our new-found skill
We bring with venturous hand,
To stand beside the marvels brought
From many an ancient land.
And as we greet each welcome guest with
grateful hearts we sing,
Of all that bygone years have brought and
coming years shall bring.

A SONG OF THE FUTURE

O Land of Hope! Thy hills aflame
Proclaim the dawn of days of fame ;
The winds that sway the forests free
Sing of the pride of years to be.

The starry cross that decks thy skies
Shall watch thy gath'ring greatness rise,
Renewing on this southern strand
The glories of our Fatherland.

AUSTRALIA

HYMN

Eternal King, our fathers' God and ours!
    Guard Thou this new-born land,
And shelter us when danger lowers with Thine
    almighty hand.
Grant in the coming seasons joy, and plenty
    crowned with peace,
Bless Thou each harvest's rip'ning ears and
    bless our flocks' increase.
Beneath this southern sky inspire with souls
    aflame,
A seed to serve Thy purpose high, and praise
    Thy sacred name.
                      Amen.

Musings in the Melbourne Picture Gallery.

I

BUNYAN IN PRISON

STRANGE entertainment for a guest so rare,
A gaol for lodging and a convict's fare,
A setting rude to hold a gem so bright,
A murky lantern for so clear a light.

Yet gained the world a great advantage, when,
" A certain place, wherein there was a den,
He lighted on"—that pris'ner, mild, yet bold,
With heart all free, and thoughts no gaol
    might hold.

With fairer scenes than gleam in Dives' halls
His fancy soon would deck those prison walls;
The dungeon dark, illumed with light would
    seem
" Where, as he slept, behold, he dreamed a
    dream."

Not to the slumbers dull of pampered ease
Do angels ministrant bring dreams like these;
By love directed, these in mercy go
To prison pallets and to beds of woe.

The weary feet must climb lone Pisgah's height
Ere Canaan's glories burst upon the sight,
And sweetest notes upon the air are flung
From heartstrings, stretched almost to break-
　　ing, wrung.

Ere from the ore the precious metal came
The crucible had borne the fiercest flame,
So flowers when crushed yield best their sweet
　　perfume,
And stars shine brightest in an hour of gloom.

II

ANGUISH

ONLY a lamb that has died in the night,
When the winds were keen, and the earth
　　was white,
And fields, where in summer the daisies grow,
Were hidden in depths of the drifting snow.

When the moon shot forth through a parted
　　cloud,
And glittering gems decked the earth's pale
　　shroud,
Her cold fading beam caught the last dim ray
From the closing eyes as life passed away.

93

When the morning mists strove to hide from
     sight
The grey, tardy dawn and its murky light,
Then the old dam strove, but she strove in
     vain,
To rouse the sleeper that woke not again.

O wintry and chill is the wind that blows,
But gathering near are the carrion crows,
And the old sheep guards with a mother's pain
Her lamb's lifeless corse on the snowy plain.

Vain, vain, alas! is her guardian care;
We know, while we pity her deep despair,
The fields, when in summer the daisies blow,
No trace of her frolicsome lamb shall know.

Yet strangely transfigured by grief and love,
By the kindred pangs that all fond hearts move,
She stands in her woe, o'er her firstborn slain,
In a regal mantle of love and pain.

And so strangely human the light that lies
In the anguished depths of those pleading eyes,
So like to our love is her vain appeal,
And so like her grief to the pangs we feel,

That our hearts go forth with a pitying dread
To the mother mourning her first-born dead,
Standing in anguish amidst the snow,
Guarding her dead from the carrion crow.

THE FIRST SNOW

From our summer lodge on the mountain
 height
 Down to the valley we go,
For the pastures green, and the flowerets
 bright
 Are hiding beneath the snow.

Gladly we welcome the beacon white
 That points us back to the vale,
And the first fair shower of snowflakes light
 As a homeward call we hail.

Fondly we watched, from the peaks above,
 Our homes in the vale below,
And oft as we thought of the friends we love
 We longed for the signal snow.

We longed for the faces loved so well,
 The sound of each well known voice,
And the music sweet of the vesper bell
 That soon shall our hearts rejoice.

There's a bliss in meeting those we love
 Which only the parted know,
So we gladly haste from the hills above
 At the first white fall of snow.

IV

DRUIDICAL MONUMENTS

Dark and dim, these mists all hoary
Well befit the shadowy glory
Round these forms majestic clinging
    In their silent solitude;
From long buried ages bringing
    Mem'ries wild of ancient days,
When in stately bands appearing,
Here their mystic altars rearing,
    Singing loud in Wodin's praise
        Came our fathers, wild and rude.

In the starlight, half revealing,
'Midst the shadows, half concealing
All the scene so weird and eerie,
    Figures priestly seem to stray;
And the moorland, wild and dreary,
    Wakes to life and song once more,
While the dark mists, slow uptending,
From these ancient shrines ascending,
    Mock the incense that of yore
        From these altars passed away.

But by pearly wings of morning,
(Rosy tints the skies adorning),
All these gloomy shades are banished
    As the nightbirds homeward fly.
But the mystic pageant vanished

Fills our soul with strange unrest,
For no garish ray of noonlight,
Nor the silv'ry gleam of moonlight,
 Can reveal the secrets prest
 To the heart of days gone by.

V

THE PILGRIM FATHERS

" AND after prayer, performed by our pastor, where a flood of tears
was poured out, they accompanied us to the ship, but were not able
to speak one to another for the abundance of sorrow to part. But
we only going on board (the ship lying to the quay and ready to set
sail, the wind being fair) we gave them a volley of small shot and
three pieces of ordnance, and so, lifting our hands to each other, and
our hearts for each other, to the Lord our God, we departed, and
found His presence with us in the 'midst of our manifold straits. He
carried us through."—*The Pilgrim Fathers.—Robinson.*

DEAR to our hearts our native land,
 Our friends, our fathers' graves,
And yet we seek a foreign strand,
 A home beyond the waves.

Bound to our hearts by many ties
 By love's soft fingers wrought,
The ground wherein each lost love lies,
 For which our fathers fought.

Dear to our hearts each flower, we feel,
 That decks the English sod,
But dearer still the right to kneel,
 As freemen, to our God.

97   F

And though our tears in vain we hide,
Though manly cheeks shall pale,
When from her shores our ships shall glide
Before the fav'ring gale,

Still in the Lord shall be our strength,
He us shall carry through,
Be with us all our journey's length,
A helper strong and true.

By His good grace, beyond the sea
A home we yet shall raise,
A newer England, yet more free,
Wherein our God to praise.

Temperance Hymns and Poems

PROLOGUE

Written for the International Temperance Conference, held during the currency of the Melbourne Exhibition, 1880

A THOUSAND flags are waving
In the golden sunlight fair;
A thousand voices ringing
In the balmy summer air.
To deck thy fane, O Labour,
Came those flags across the sea,
And like "sound of many waters"
Are those voices raised to thee.

We hear the anthems swelling
In the courts to Labour raised,
And list glad voices telling
How fair Art may best be praised.
We hail thee, Art and Labour!
And we join the gladsome throng
Who surround thy pleasant altars
With the jovial voice of song.

We seek to take no banner
From the many that are thine,
Nor still the voice of singing
That is heard around thy shrine.
We would but on thine altars
Lay one chaplet, sweet and rare,

F2

That shall add a strength to Labour,
And shall render Art more fair.

We'll weave our votive garland,
In this dewy dawn of time
That views an Empire rising
In a golden southern clime,
Of flowers and gems of promise
That shall cast a brighter ray
Than the silv'ry gleam of moonlight
Or the glaring eye of day.

For Joy and Peace and Plenty
In our Temperance wreath shall twine,
While Faith and Love and Freedom
With a purer ray shall shine.
Its leaves no more shall wither,
For the truth must ever stand,
And the incense of their sweetness
Shall perfume our Southern Land.

A clearer light shall beckon
Art's votaries on their way;
Our toilers shall be stronger
Freed from Drink's enfeebling sway;
Our altars shall be fairer,
And our homes more blest shall be,
When from chains of Drink's oppression
Shall the truth make all men free.

ALMIGHTY FRIEND

ALMIGHTY Friend, Thy smile we see
Reflected in the sunlit sea;
The earth beneath, the sky above,
Thine impress bear of changeless love;
With light and peace around us shed
And flowers about our pathway spread,
Would men but heed Thy righteous will,
The world would be an Eden still.

But tears and anguish, shame and woe,
Ever from Sin's dread fountain flow;
The luring wiles by Satan spread
Where heedless thousands idly tread,
The red wine's gleam, the syren's strain,
Their victims bind in guilt's dark chain;
Hurled o'er Temptation's treach'rous brink
Beneath Destruction's wave they sink.

Eternal Love! We seek Thine aid,
Against the powers of Sin arrayed;
Help us, through Christ, who died to save
The soul of man from death's cold grave,
To break the Drunkard's bond of pain,
To lead him home to Thee again,
And free these fair Australian lands
From Sin's despite and Sorrow's bands.

THE SONS OF RECHAB

A REVERIE

Written for the Jubilee Celebration of the Independent Order of Rechabites in 1885

BACK through the ages! Pass with reverent feet
  Between the tombs where sleep the mighty
    dead;
Lift up the curtains of the bygone years,
  The phantom cities of the past we'll tread.

· · · · · · · ·

How fair stands Zion's Hill! The Temple gates
  Invite our entrance. There the tribes repair
For holy worship. Hark! the voice of song
  Is sweetly heralding the hour of prayer.

· · · · · · · ·

What stately forms are these appearing now,
  Whose garb and tongue betray an alien
    race?
Have Rechab's sons come up their vows to
    pay,
  Or in His courts to seek Jehovah's face?

Though "praise is comely," they come not to
    sing,
  Nor seek the altar, though 'tis well to pray.
To each his office. They are here to serve
  The God of Heav'n in His appointed way.

They come to testify; but not before
  The great assembly. Things in secret done
God's voice can publish. Not alone on fields
  'Midst pomp of war are noblest vict'ries won.

There is a chamber which o'erlooks the gate,
  Thither they enter, by the prophet led.
Why stand they wond'ring? Through the
    stately room
  The subtle fragrance of the vine is shed.

"Drink! 'Tis God's house and 'tis His
    prophet calls."
  Strange, that the tempter thus should come,
    and here!
How shall the desert's untaught sons reply,
  What answer give for God and men to hear?

There is no power that like a simple faith
  Can reach the right when gathering doubts
    prevail :

No weapon find we that can equal Truth
   For man to trust to when all others fail.

"' Drink ye no wine.' 'Twas thus our father
     spoke—
"' Build ye no houses, and no vineyards till,
"' But dwell in tents amidst the desert sands.'
  " His voice our law, and we obey it still."

Then came the word of the approving God,
   The Lord of Hosts, the God of Israel's race,
" Thy father's seed for ever shall endure,
  " Nor want a man to stand before my face."

    .   .   .   .

Upon our shoulders, in these later days,
   The vows which bound those faithful sons
     we take,
And equal blessing from our God we crave,
   Not for ourselves, but for our cause's sake.

This is our prayer :—That ne'er through coming
     years
'Midst any people or in any clime,
A man be wanting who shall dare to stand
   For Truth and Temperance, to the end of
     Time.

THE VICTORIAN ALLIANCE HYMN

I

GOD of Love! In mercy hear us,
While before Thy throne we bend!
Holy Spirit! hov'ring near us,
    Now Thy gracious influence lend.
With Thy love our souls inspire,
Touch our lips with sacred fire;
In the strife that lies before us,
Spread the victor's banner o'er us.

II

Fount of all the hopes we cherish,
Christ, who died our race to save;
Help us, for the souls who perish,
    Ev'ry hostile foe to brave.
Arm, O arm us for the fight,
Gird us with celestial might;
'Midst the strife to guide and cheer us,
May we feel Thy presence near us.

III

In the war that knows no ceasing,
Waged by powers of Heaven and Hell,
May our armies, still increasing,
    Bear the brunt of battle well.

That from Drink's dread thrall set free,
This fair southern land may be;
Aid us in the bold endeavour,
From our shores this curse to sever.

IV

Now Thy plenteous mercies show'ring,
Grant an answer to our prayer;
That when threatening ills are low'ring,
    Thou Thy mighty arm wilt bare.
All our hopes on Thee we place,
All our trust is in Thy grace;
In the strife that lies before us,
Spread thy conqu'ring banner o'er us.

THE VICTORIAN ALLIANCE WAR SONG

WE are fighting for the freedom
    Of our land from Drink's dread chain,
For the cleansing of her banner
    From its dark, degrading stain.
And our God Himself shall lead us
    Till our times of warfare cease,
And the day of Prohibition
    Ushers in the reign of Peace.

There are anxious eyes now watching
  For the dawning of that day;
There are weary souls now waiting,
  There are trembling lips that pray;
There are weak ones heavy laden
  With the drunkard's load of pain;
There are fond hearts sadly mourning
  O'er the dear ones Drink has slain.

'Tis our hope to raise the fallen,
  'Tis our joy the weak to save,
We would shield the frail and tempted
  From the drunkard's hopeless grave;
And our eyes are on the future,
  On the brighter days to be,
For a sober, godly nation
  In a land from Drink set free.

Gather, gather round our standard
  All who love this southern land,
Who would have it in the forefront
  Of the World's great Nations stand!
Gather, gather round our standard!
  Thus in Freedom's name we call,
That our Land may find redemption
  From the Drink-fiend's fatal thrall.

A HYMN

When brightest sunbeams o'er my head shall
    shine,
And Earth's fair blossoms round my footsteps
    twine,
When glitt'ring treasures at my feet are laid,
Amidst the glare, O Christ, be Thou my Shade.

When 'neath chill blasts the garlands fade and
    die,
And quenched with tears Earth's festal torches
    lie,
When all my path is veiled in starless night,
Amidst the gloom, O Christ, be Thou my Light.

Be Thou my Shield, my Guard on fields of strife,
My Guiding Star o'er trackless waves of life,
My Port of Refuge and my destined End,
My God, my Saviour, my abiding Friend.

Through life my Hope, in death my only Stay;
O'er shifting sands of Time my steadfast Way;
My Balm when stricken, and my Song when
    blest,
My Staff, my Crown, and my Eternal Rest.

AUSTRALIAN TEMPERANCE HYMN.

Eternal King, whose love benign,
On earth each perfect blessing pours,
We fain would see more truly Thine
These southern lands, these fertile shores;
Thine are the precious things that fill
These coasts with plenty and with glee,
The cattle on each grassy hill,
The harvest field, the woodland free.

The orchard's wealth, the clust'ring vine,
The fragrant herb, the wild bird's song,
The hoarded treasures of the mine,
All to Thy bounteous hand belong;
The stars that gleam in cloudless skies,
The golden sunshine's cheering ray,
Each beauty that around us lies,
Owe all their being to Thy sway.

All these Thy law's demands fulfil,
At Thy command they come and go;
Man only, with presumptuous will,
Dares a rebellious face to show;
Or bound in chains of low desire,
Turns from Thy courts, so fair and free,
To seek, from some unholy fire,
The light that comes alone from Thee.

Help us Thy banner high to rear,
Of Truth and Temperance loud to sing,
That men the message glad may hear,
And own allegiance to their King ;
May dwell beside this southern main
A people zealous in Thy cause,
And freed from Drink's ensnaring chain,
Obedient to Thy righteous laws.

VOTE AS YOU PRAY

YE friends of the Lord, we beseech you,
  Vote as you pray!
O list to your hearts! They will teach you,
  Vote as you pray!
Vote for the kingdom of glory and peace,
Vote that the evil amongst us may cease,
Vote that things holy and pure may increase,
  Vote as you pray!

A power is yours, will you use it ?
  Vote as you pray!
A privilege vast, don't abuse it,
  Vote as you pray!
Vote that the tempted in safety may tread,
Vote that the drunkard from evil be led,
His children be clothed, the hungry be fed.
  Vote as you pray!

FAREWELL

SWEET friend, farewell!
It was "the Master's voice"
That called thee hence,
So we would fain rejoice ;
And yet with tears, with bitter tears,
We say, " Farewell."

So early called!
Too late we know thy worth,
And on the silence feel how sweet
The music of thy life on earth,
And miss thy voice, the voice
We hear no more.

Sweet friend, farewell!
No friend that loved thee best,
Nor those thou lov'dst, would dare
To call thee from thy Saviour's breast,
Altho' with tears, with bitter tears,
We say " Farewell."

MELBOURNE:

McCARRON, BIRD & CO., PRINTERS,

479 COLLINS STREET.